She Stoops
to Comedy

David Greenspan

A SAMUEL FRENCH ACTING EDITION

FOUNDED 1830

SAMUELFRENCH.COM
SAMUELFRENCH-LONDON.CO.UK

FOR PRODUCTION ENQUIRIES

UNITED STATES AND CANADA
Info@SamuelFrench.com
1-866-598-8449

UNITED KINGDOM AND EUROPE
Theatre@SamuelFrench-London.co.uk
020-7255-4302

Each title is subject to availability from Samuel French, depending upon country of performance. Please be aware that SHE STOOPS TO COMEDY may not be licensed by Samuel French in your territory. Professional and amateur producers should contact the nearest Samuel French office or licensing partner to verify availability.

MUSIC USE NOTE

Licensees are solely responsible for obtaining formal written permission from copyright owners to use copyrighted music in the performance of this play and are strongly cautioned to do so. If no such permission is obtained by the licensee, then the licensee must use only original music that the licensee owns and controls. Licensees are solely responsible and liable for all music clearances and shall indemnify the copyright owners of the play(s) and their licensing agent, Samuel French, against any costs, expenses, losses and liabilities arising from the use of music by licensees. Please contact the appropriate music licensing authority in your territory for the rights to any incidental music.

IMPORTANT BILLING AND CREDIT REQUIREMENTS

If you have obtained performance rights to this title, please refer to your licensing agreement for important billing and credit requirements.

SHE STOOPS TO COMEDY had its world premiere produced by Playwrights Horizons at the Peter Jay Sharp Theater in New York, NY on April 3, 2003. The production was directed by David Greenspan, with sets by Michael Brown, costumes by Miranda Hoffman, and lighting by Matthew Frey. The Production Stage Manager was Beth Stiegel-Rohr. The cast was as follows:

ALEXANDRA PAGE	David Greenspan
ALISON ROSE	Marissa Copeland
KAY FEIN/ JAYNE SUMMERHOUSE	E. Katherine Kerr
HAL STEWART	Philip Tabor
EVE ADDAMAN	Mia Barron
SIMON LANQUISH	T. Ryder Smith

CHARACTERS

ALEXANDRA PAGE – an actress, assumes the role of Harry Samson

ALISON ROSE – Alexandra's lover, also an actress

KAY FEIN – close friend of Alexandra, an archeologist or a lighting designer

HAL STEWART – a filmmaker

EVE ADDAMAN – Hal's girlfriend – also a filmmaker

JAYNE SUMMERHOUSE – rival to Alexandra, also an actress, she's studying filmmaking.

SIMON LANQUISH – an actor

SETTING

The stage of course.

TIME

As indicated.

AUTHOR'S NOTES

Alexandra Page is played by an actor, not an actress. At no time in the play is that actor in drag.

A cast of six. One actress plays Kay Fein and Jayne Summerhouse.

A bed. Four stools. Legs down left and right that serve as off stage. Cell phones should be mimed.

Alexandra should be visible during her first "off-stage" scene in the bathroom. During the final scene, she must be out of sight, truly off stage prior to her entrance.

The actors must never "step out" of character to comment on the play. They must remain in character and in the play when faced with incongruities or sudden "revisions."

ALEX. The urge then to move across the words the page to paint a character on the stage.

The impulse then to translate onto the stage. The stage I say as fast as flexible as the page.

This then to make through revision the stage a play of words moving its characters its plot its action.

Okay fine you say so what a comedy perhaps not funny. Words then you see as you hear them not always connected but enough. This is the way I'll do it.

An actress, name: Alexandra Page. Her lover, Alison Rose. An actress also. Alexandra Page and Alison Rose. This is not funny. Okay, fine. Kay – Fein. Their friend, Kay Fein. Alex's friend, Kay Fein. An archeologist just back from a dig. A room with curtains and a bed and a door and an offstage. Okay. Fine. Talk, Kay. Talk, Kay Fein.

KAY. Alex, what're you doing?

ALEX. What am *I* doing? What're *you* doing? I mean here. I thought you were on a dig.

KAY. I was. I'm back. What're you doing in there?

ALEX. I'm changing. I'll be right out. I was shocked to get your call, Kay. Shocked. Where were you again?

KAY. In Egypt. I was in Egypt. You know, the usual stuff. My hands filthy with the past. Ancient history under my fingernails. And then that call from Charlotte – at my hotel – in Cairo – that you and Alison had split up.

ALEX. And you dropped everything?

KAY. I rushed to London, I flew to New York.

ALEX. You flew?

KAY. Well this is 1950.

ALEX. How fast we move – the modern age. And yet at times, Kay, it all feels so post-modern. Whatever that means.

KAY. Well, if it doesn't mean anything now, it will probably mean something then.

ALEX. I don't know how it happened. Oh, Kay. A fight, of course. One of the many. I too am an actress. That's her talking. I had just gotten back from the coast. A small part in a big picture. After all these years on the stage, but I am a stage creature – a creature of the stage – and film, you know, the motion picture – I mean what does it do for me? What does it – what has it done for me? Hope Court had a tiny role a cameo, precious little Hope – and Laurence Lawrence – after that scandal in the men's room – you naughty boy I told him he wasn't amused. And Hal, a man of the theatre or so he says, now he's making pictures, trying to make it in pictures – I played his sister's best friend. I was horrid – to everyone. Abysmal. And the food! Well, I got home –

KAY. I got home after the dig in Egypt and Charlotte told me that you and Alison had split up.

ALEX. She told you what?

KAY. She said she heard from Jayne Summerhouse –

ALEX. Jayne Summerhouse? Foreshadowing.

KAY. That you and Alison had split up.

ALEX. Who said that, Jayne said that? That's ridiculous. No. We had words, yes, but that has nothing to do with the fact that Alison is not in this scene. Alison was cast in *As You Like It.*

KAY. The one by Shakespeare?

ALEX. I think so. We fought about what? I don't remember these things. Her not spending enough time with me. She's been taking this acting class. We were arguing about the kitty litter. It hadn't been changed. In days. It was her fault. Clearly. Or maybe it was my day to do it. It's of no importance. We were fighting and she said

I didn't I wasn't interested enough in her career. I too am an actress, that's her talking. And anyway she left for Maine, someplace in Maine – don't come unless I call you it may be horrible and I don't want you to see it and tell me and then their Orlando was arrested. Some incident in a men's room – I don't ask for details – the naughty boy.

KAY. I hear that Hal is directing *As You Like It*.

ALEX. Which is not how he likes it. The movie was a bomb. His three-picture deal is kaput.

KAY. Some place in Maine, I hear.

ALEX. There's no place in Maine, believe me, I've been there. Some avant-garde take I guess on the play. A post-modern spin.

KAY. Well this is 1990.

ALEX. And you know Hal. Don't you?

KAY. He's a film director, isn't he?

ALEX. Small independent films. I had a role in one, one scene against Humé Hubert, this young French Canadian actor with a speech impediment. He's gonna be a major star.

KAY. I don't understand what's going on, Alex. Stay in the present. Leave the past to me.

ALEX. Kay, it's simple. I did this film – it was how many years ago I don't remember – 1995 or 4 or 3. So it was about two years ago. This is 1997. I guess I was awful because they cut me and replaced me with another actress. I had this one scene opposite the lead, Humé Hubert.

KAY. The young French Canadian actor with a speech impediment? I hear he's going to be a major star.

ALEX. That's the one. Anyway the actress I guess they replaced me with was believe it or not worse than I was – or something – they said I wasn't speaking to rest of the picture – whatever the fuck that means – but then this actress they got – I don't know what happened. Somehow or other I ended up back in the film.

KAY. I like Hal's movies, he's kind of avant-garde. Whatever that means these days.

ALEX. It means nothing. The avant-garde is over. Or at least it is for me. But he's not avant – garde – he's just – he just has taste, he's intelligent. He's not spelling the whole thing out. You do that – and if you're somewhat intellectual, not just intelligent but intellectual – you're considered avant-garde. Don't ask me. And you're not, you never were. And he's never directed a play before and he has some ideas, I guess about a play doing a play a Shakespeare play like a film because Shakespeare I think he feels practically invented the cinema. Whatever that means. I don't care it sounds interesting and Alison – who has spent years too many years in one revival of *Oklahoma* or *Carousel* – I mean for god's sake, how many times can you be a cock-eyed optimist in Pittsburgh – don't get me wrong I like those things – or at least I liked the albums – one revival after the other and for Alison to have a chance to play Rosalind I mean she met Hal at a dinner party for the film I was in and cut from and then put back into and he liked her and he read her and he cast her and he didn't cast me didn't even audition me but that's all right, I understand.

KAY. Alex. Pause. So she's cast as Rosalind, that's exciting.

ALEX. It's thrilling. And she's a nervous wreck. I was coaching her, we were fighting, I was jealous, she was nervous, we were fighting and now she's fine. She left for Maine, they lost an actor – Hubert. He was playing Orlando.

KAY. The young French Canadian actor with a speech impediment.

ALEX. Naturally. Well we all knew he'd be a major star. He's in L.A. Doing something.

KAY. But Alex let's go back.

ALEX. How far?

KAY. 1970?

ALEX. Oh, Kay!

KAY. For atmosphere, not continuity.

ALEX. Well just for a moment.

KAY. I mean your career.

ALEX. My career?

KAY. The roles you've played, Alex. Hedda, Phaedra.

ALEX. *(Fehdra)* Phaedra. 1998. We're back.

KAY. Just recently, three Phaedras.

ALEX. *(Fehdras)* Phaedras. Four of them – those two modern adaptations – one of them set on the moon for christ sake all of us wearing those stupid space suits – aha-haah – then the Euripides finally the Racine. I'm fed up with Phaedra – why doesn't she just get over it.

KAY. Cleopatra, Clythemnestra.

ALEX. All out of town – of course. Except for the one on the moon. How embarrassing. And for no money. She left on Saturday. They begin rehearsal on Tuesday.

KAY. In Maine?

ALEX. Some shed near a pond. Heavens, the mosquitoes. Poor Hal, losing Humé on such short notice. Hell, I'd play the part. I'm so tired of the roles I get cast in. These angry, depressed women. Why do people think I'm so angry? I'm not angry. For god fucking sake. I'm not depressed. Today. I'd love to play Orlando.

KAY. Audition.

ALEX. What?

KAY. I'm kidding.

ALEX. *(with a bray of laughter)* I should audition, shouldn't I?

KAY. Cut your hair, put on a suit or something and show up.

ALEX. Right. Like I could pull that off. With my figure. I've gotta lose some weight.

KAY. Well, finish getting dressed, I'll take you out for breakfast.

ALEX. Thanks. Phone rings.

KAY. Hello. Oh hi, Seymour, it's Kay. Alex, it's your agent.

ALEX. I'll be right out.

KAY. No, she's changing. Metamorphosing. Well, you know her, the bathroom is her temple. She makes obeisance to the gods. No, I just got back into town. No, that was an earlier draft, I'm no longer an archeologist, I'm a lighting designer. I was in Cleveland. *The Matchmaker*, *Salesman*. Minneapolis. The Molnar play – the funny one – and then something else – I can't remember the names anymore – it all seems like one endless play. No, I loved it – sort of. *Oedipus*. Yes, but that's months away. In two weeks. Kind of vacation. In Maine. But then I'm lighting – you know Hal Stewart? The film director, right. He's doing *As You Like It*. Yes, Alison. She's fine, she's nervous. Hysterical that's she's going to be alone.

ALEX. I'm not hysterical.

KAY. Sure. Oh, she'll love that. 'Bye love. He said call him tomorrow. They're doing *Hamlet* in Buffalo. They wanna see you for the Ghost.

ALEX. You're kidding!

KAY. Alex, I'm bewildered. What is it with the contemporary theatre? This penchant for cross-dressing. Men around the cauldron. Noras with five o'clock shadow. It's the year 2000, but I mean really.

(Enter **ALEXANDRA** *disguised as a man.)*

ALEX. It's funny, isn't it.

KAY. Yes and –

*(***KAY** *turns, sees. Screams.)*

Oh, my god, who are you? Alex. Alex, there's a man.

ALEX. Kay, it's me.

KAY. Don't you come near me or I'll......Alex?

ALEX. What do you think?

KAY. You're not serious.

ALEX. Of course I am.

KAY. I see it all.

ALEX. I thought you would.

KAY. You're…"changing." Orlando.

ALEX. First I have to audition. Think I'll get it?

KAY. *(stunned)* You look like a man.

ALEX. I told Hal, after I read the script I told him I said, I'd love to audition. He said, no, I know your work from Jeff's play. I said, Okay, but I've never done a film before. Expanded the role when he thought of me. Cut me all the same. Now I audition.

KAY. Your hair!

ALEX. Does it look too butch. I hate those dykey cuts.

KAY. You cut your hair and dyed it.

ALEX. Dyed it? I had the dye taken out. Did you really think I was a red-head?

KAY. After all these years. Have I been so deceived?

ALEX. Kay, I am an actress. Please keep that in mind.

KAY. I feel like I hardly know you.

ALEX. It's just a costume. A few odds and ends.

KAY. Where are your breasts? What's that between your legs?

ALEX. Surely you've seen one of these before.

KAY. Not on you.

ALEX. There's a open call at 1:00. It's amazing what you can do with a little spirit gum and an Ace bandage.

KAY. You have a cock.

ALEX. *(holding it)* Wanna touch it.

KAY. *(recoiling)* Ahahaah!

ALEX. It's just chicken wire and polyester stuffing.

KAY. Where'd you get all that hair?

ALEX. *(arms, legs and chest)* It's Laurence Olivier's.

KAY. *(disbelieving)* Alexandra Page!

ALEX. He always shaved his legs for roles in tights. I got it from this guy in my building.

KAY. Would you be real.

ALEX. I am. The hair on my ass once belonged to Vivian Leigh.

KAY. You're going to audition for the role of Orlando. But why the anatomy?

ALEX. I'm not taking any chances. Remember the wrestling scene? Who knows what I'll be asked to do.

KAY. But Alex, do you really think you can pull this off? And what's your motivation for all this?

ALEX. How the hell should I know? Oh please don't examine the script too closely, Kay, we'll all be in trouble. Jealousy. Rivalry. I don't know. Look at a re-run of *Lucy*. I'm grabbing at straws. Why did she do half those things? Jayne Summerhouse. There you go. She's a treat – I mean a threat. It was a typo.

KAY. Jayne of course, she had a thing with Alison years ago.

ALEX. A thing *for* Alison.

KAY. Or so you tell yourself.

ALEX. Well, there you have it, motivation. I don't want Alison to sleep with Jayne Summerhouse. Or the fact that all I do is play tragic women in creepy modern adaptations. Blanche in a bathtub, Beckett in a tube stop, Congreve at the corner saloon.

KAY. Oh, stop acting.

ALEX. I will not. I love it. I love to act. And when I do get a chance to play one of those roles straight, it's in some boring production with some dweepy director who doesn't know the difference between convention and the conventional. No life! And I'm tired of it. I just wanna have some fun for god's sake. I'm tired of sitting on my ass.

KAY. Well there's your motivation.

ALEX. Huh? Right! Fine, whatever. And don't get me started on new plays. What I think of some of those. We'll get to that later. What was the question?

KAY. I don't remember.

ALEX. Do you think you can pull this off?

KAY. Right.

ALEX. I don't give a damn. The worst that can happen is I'm discovered. Uncovered. Another masquerade. Well, so what, it's my nature. I'm not afraid.

KAY. But sweetie can you act – really act – like a man?

ALEX. Oh man, man. Woman, woman. What's the difference?

KAY. There is a difference. I mean you look like a man. But can you play the part? And I'm not talking from a distance, when you're on the stage painted with light. I mean in the flesh. Can you convince those in life, convince yourself?

ALEX. I don't have to convince anybody, darling. That shit is for amateurs. The whole world's a fucking drag show. Look at them, they're all in costume. I'm not playing anything. I'm not acting. I'm not pretending. I don't have to act like a man. I don't know what a man is, or a woman. What is man? What is woman? Who in their right mind knows? Go back to Egypt. Dig! I guess you're an archeologist again. See what you find. I'm off to Arden. And why the hell not?

(Enter HAL, EVE and ALISON. Exit KAY.)

HAL. Sorry to keep you waiting. I'm Hal.

ALEX. *(her hairy arms)* I'm hairy. Samson. Harry Samson.

HAL. Harry?

ALEX. Samson. Harry Samson.

HAL. Well thanks for coming in. This is my assistant, Eve.

ALEX. Eve?

EVE. Addaman.

ALEX. Addaman?

EVE. Eve. Eve Addaman.

ALEX. Eve Addaman.

HAL. And this is our Rosalind, Alison Rose.

ALEX. Alison?

ALISON. Alison. Alison Rose.

HAL. Alison's Rosalind.

ALISON. Alison Rose.

ALEX. Rosalind.

ALISON. Alison.

ALEX. Alison.

EVE. Rosalind. Rosalind's Alison.

HAL. Alison Rose.

ALEX. Eve. Hal. Harry. Samson. Alison Rose. Alison's Rosalind. Alison Rose.

HAL. I think you've got it.

ALEX. It's nice to meet you.

HAL. Just give us a minute to get organized.

ALEX. Sure.

    (exit **ALISON***)*

HAL. We'll start with the opening speech to Adam.

ALEX. Okay.

HAL. Then look at the scene between you and Rosalind.

ALEX. Right.

HAL. *(to* **EVE***)* Can we get rid of this bed?

EVE. Sure.

HAL. *(to* **ALEX***)* Looks like someone just finished a production of *Cat on a Hot Tin Roof.*

ALEX. *(with reference to the bed, chortling)* Oh right.

HAL. You know the play?

ALEX. Done it – twice.

HAL. Play Brick?

ALEX. Not really.

HAL. *(to* **EVE***)* Actually, you know, why don't you why don't we leave it, that way there's something to sit on.

EVE. Okay.

HAL. *(to* **ALEX***)* You have a picture, resumé?

ALEX. No, actually, I don't. I just got back into town, haven't unpacked my stuff. I just ran down here when I heard you were seeing people.

HAL. That's all right, we know what you look like. Where have you been…

ALEX. Working?

HAL. Yea.

ALEX. Are you familiar with theatres in Montana at all?

HAL. Nope.

ALEX. Yea, I've spent a lot of time last few years working in Montana. At the uh Montana Rep.

HAL. Great.

ALEX. Yea.

HAL. Who's directing up there?

ALEX. Directing? Oh…you know, what's her name – my god I've worked with her for years I can't believe I – Levi. Simple. Levi Simple.

HAL. Name is familiar.

ALEX. Yea, he's been – she's been – he's been up there… since the beginning.

HAL. What kind of stuff they do?

ALEX. Did *The Guardsman* – old Lunt/Fontaine vehicle. That was fun – farce, kind of. Um…*Biff at Colonus.* Kind of an experimental piece – didn't really pan out – interesting idea, though. And then just your… standard stuff, usual stuff…that gets done…across the country…all the time…Everywhere.

HAL. Well great. And here's Alison.

(enter ALISON)

ALISON. Sorry. Sorry. I got stuck in traffic. The trains.

HAL. No problem. We've got one more audition. If you don't mind waiting.

ALISON. No.

HAL. *(to ALEX)* This is Alison Rose. She's playing Rosalind.

ALEX. Hi, nice to meet you. I'm Harry. Samson. Harry Samson.

ALISON. Hi.

(*Long handshake, they look at each other.*)

HAL. So give us a minute. (*to* **EVE**, *surreptitiously*) Interesting chemistry between them.

(**ALEX** *and* **ALISON** *finally let go hands.*)

ALEX. (*off long handshake*) Oh, sorry. Must be a little nervous.

ALISON. That's all right, don't be. Is this your first time doing Shakespeare?

ALEX. Oh, no, un, no, I've uh, done a little. Not too much. Quite a lot.

ALISON. Then I'm the one that should be nervous.

ALEX. Why do you say that?

ALISON. My first role, really. In Shakespeare. In a Shakespeare.

ALEX. Huh. You've been doing…

ALISON. Musicals mostly. Mostly musicals. Musical comedy.

ALEX. Musical comedy?

ALISON. Musical comedy. Musical theatre, musical comedy. Musical comedy.

ALEX. Musical comedy.

ALISON. Did *Pygmalion* – not too long ago. A few years ago. In high school.

ALEX. Oh, right, sure.

ALISON. Shaw.

ALEX. Right.

ALISON. *My Fair Lady*. That was interesting. But mostly… musical…comedy.

ALEX. Musical comedy.

ALISON. Musical theatre, musical comedy. Musical comedy.

ALEX. I'm sure you'll do fine.

ALISON. Hope so. You've been…

ALEX. Out of town lately a lot. Just got back in really – going back out again – I hope – if I get...

ALISON. What brought you back?

ALEX. What?

ALISON. What brought you back?

ALEX. Well, I uh split up with someone, recently. Woman I was living with.

ALISON. Oh really? Me too.

ALEX. Yea. What?

ALISON. I haven't told – well, yet. It's terrible I know, I just figure this summer, get some space – I can...you know.

ALEX. God. I'm shocked. About how hard it is when you –

ALISON. Breaking up?

ALEX. Yea. Yes. I mean for me.

ALISON. Really? Did she break up with you or did you break up with her? I guess it's always kind of a mutual thing whether you know it or not. I mean you saw it coming, yes?

ALEX. No. Not really. No. I was – it was kind of a...I was kind of you know...shocked I guess.

ALISON. You were – were you married?

ALEX. Yes. No. I mean for all intents and purposes.

ALISON. Same with us. We lived together for years. Did she work in the theatre?

ALEX. In a way. Kind of...depends on what you think theatre is.

ALISON. What do you mean?

ALEX. What do I mean? It's difficult to say – at this moment – but uh. What about the uh...Boy this is an old draft, isn't it?

ALISON. It sure is.

ALEX. This breaking up stuff, I completely forgot about the man you were with? Was he –

ALISON. A woman.

ALEX. I'm sorry?

ALISON. A woman. He was a woman. Is a woman.

ALEX. Oh, I'm sorry. I mean about –

ALISON. And she does – it's all right – works in the theatre.

ALEX. Wasn't working…

ALISON. Out between us? No. But she doesn't know I mean I haven't told her yet but I told you that I didn't, didn't I?

ALEX. I think so.

ALISON. And you've been working –

ALEX. Out of town mostly. Going back out again – I hope – if I get –

ALISON. What…what brought you back?

ALEX. I've been just tired of what I'd been doing. Kind of getting into a rut and I thought I'd just kind of mix things up a bit trying something new I hadn't done before. Plus my girlfriend is uh I don't know you know what I mean she's doing something for the summer in a show and so my agent got a call about a…well, you know what I mean.

ALISON. Sort of.

ALEX. It's tough – relationships.

ALISON. In a way. In a way. She's very self-involved.

ALEX. Your girlfriend.

ALISON. Lover.

ALEX. Ex-lover.

ALISON. Right. She's always reminding me – everyone in fact – that we're not girlfriends we're lovers, that we're not girls anymore.

ALEX. I see her point.

ALISON. But it's very annoying. Kind of pretentious the way she says it. Correcting people all the time about it. Somewhat arrogant.

ALEX. Did you ever tell her that?

ALISON. I can't remember. What about the woman you were with?

ALEX. Was she self-involved?

ALISON. No, I mean –

ALEX. Yes, in her own way. In her own quiet way. Has a way though of making it appear as though I'm the one that's self-involved. When in truth we both are.

ALISON. Interesting.

ALEX. Yes. But you were going to say?

ALISON. Nothing. Nothing.

ALEX. Your ex-lover anyone I might know?

ALISON. You might. Actually, though, I'd rather not...

ALEX. Oh, sure, sorry.

ALISON. It's fine. I was kind of blabbing.

ALEX. Should be – shouldn't be getting involved with – in other people's situations.

ALISON. Don't worry about it.

ALEX. Problem I have.

ALISON. It's all right. We'd probably have a lot to talk about.

ALEX. I'm sure we would. Who knows? Maybe we'll...

HAL. Hey, guys – I'm wondering – Alison would you mind if it's okay with Harry, how would you guys feel about reading a scene together?

ALEX. Love it.

ALISON. Okay.

HAL. Great, well welcome to Maine.

ALEX. Thank you.

HAL. You guys come up together?

ALISON. We were on the same train but didn't know it.

HAL. You're kidding.

ALEX. Yea.

HAL. That's wild.

ALISON. We shared a taxi from the station.

HAL. You guys come up together?

ALEX. We were on the same train but didn't know it.

ALISON. I didn't even know he was cast.

HAL. We didn't call you?

ALISON. No.

ALEX. We shared a taxi from the station, got acquainted a bit more. Dropped off our stuff at the hotel.

HAL. Great. Okay. It's gonna be great. I'm so excited. I'm really excited, think you guys are going to be great together. Going to be explosive.

ALEX. Oh yea.

ALISON. This is the theatre.

HAL. It is. Now.

ALISON. It's beautiful. What was it before?

HAL. It keeps changing. It's been a million things. It used to be a rehearsal hall. Before that someone lived here. Right now it's a theatre.

ALISON. Incredible.

ALEX. Theatre.

HAL. Yea.

EVE. Gotta get rid of this bed.

HAL. Oh no, leave it. I have this idea about using it. In the production.

ALEX. Really?

HAL. Oh yea. Something really kind of interesting. But… well, you'll see.

(JAYNE SUMMERHOUSE *and* SIMON LANQUISH *enter with luggage.*)

JAYNE. *(with energized, dramatic fatigue)* Hi.

HAL. You're here!

JAYNE. We got lost.

SIMON. Of course.

JAYNE. Took the wrong road. Went down the wrong path. Made the wrong turn.

SIMON. What else is new?

JAYNE. But we're here. And don't you love us for it.

ALISON. Hi Jayne.

JAYNE. Alison! I can't believe it I'm so excited. So excited. I was so excited about doing it with you. This.

ALISON. Me too.

JAYNE. Just like old times. I won't elaborate.

ALISON. Oh yea.

JAYNE. *(to the others)* We were under grad together. In the dorms. Those awful curtains. So tacky. Then me going on to grad school. In Seattle. Really getting the training I needed. It was great. I work. I've worked. And you – musical theatre. So talented. Raking in the bucks. Those national tours. I was envious. Then I got the soap. How's Alex?

ALISON. She's good. She's okay.

JAYNE. I miss her. I love her. Give her my best. Give her my love.

ALISON. I will.

JAYNE. I haven't seen you for ages.

ALISON. I know.

JAYNE. *(to ALISON)* Well you know I've been insane. I went back to school. Did you know that?

ALISON. No, I didn't.

JAYNE. Oh yes.

ALEX. For acting?

JAYNE. *(looking over ALEXANDRA)* Film school. Columbia. *(back to ALISON)* The program's incredible. The money I put away from the soap. Thank heaven that's over. It was fun. My character had a web site. But here I am. In the flesh. It's great the way this worked out. For the summer. Making a film while I'm up here. A pseudo – documentary about reality in the theatre. Hal's my mentor. I had to beg him. *(to ALEXANDRA, imperiously, offering her hand)* Who are you? I'm Jayne.

ALEX. *(accepting her hand, shaking)* I'm Harry.

JAYNE. Airy?

ALEX. Harry. Samson. Payne?

JAYNE. Jayne. Summerhouse. Are you part of the cast? Or are you one of the technical people?

HAL. Harry is our Orlando.

JAYNE. Oh, no! What happened to Hubert?

HAL. He had to drop out. *(to* **ALEXANDRA***)* Humé Hubert was going to originally be playing Orlando.

ALEX. Oh gee.

HAL. He's in L.A. Doing something.

JAYNE. I'm devastated. What's he doing? I don't want to know. He was so right. So perfect. Everything about him. Brilliant. And that unique speech pattern.

HAL. *(to* **ALEXANDRA***)* Do you know him?

ALEX. I may have worked with him – once – a while ago. I think.

HAL. Hey Simon. Let me introduce you.

JAYNE. Silent Simon. Thinking. Evaluating. Playing it cool. Keeping to himself. Maintaining a distance. Let others come to him. At first, then boom, he won't stop talking. I'm teasing, I love you. We work together always. On almost every project. It's not intentional. I don't know how it happens. Neither does he. A surprise every time. Unless we've chatted the night before. Oh my god. So am I. That's amazing. It'll be great. It'll be fun. What a blast. We'll have dinner every night. Someone to talk to. Someone to listen. The audience thinks the others can hear this and maybe they can or maybe they can't, it being kept purposely ambiguous. If they can hear it – what I'm saying – the other characters – me rattling on in this fashion, it can be interpreted either as a depiction of psychotic behavior – clearly she's insane – or given the permissiveness of theatrical artifice, an exercise in brutal satire. If, on the other hand, the speech can be heard by the audience only, what is it then but a manifestation of my inner turmoil. Satire achieved, surely, and the vague emptiness that inhibits inhabits inhibits my soul. Laugh if you must and I hope you do. I am a character in fiction. I'm meant to be funny. And I intend to be.

HAL. *(introducing* SIMON *to* ALISON*)* Do you know Alison Rose? Alison is our Rosalind. Our Ganymede.

SIMON. I think we've met. Through Alexandra Page. I was Gooper in *Cat* in Phoenix.

ALISON. Oh, I think so, yes.

JAYNE. That was one of Alex's campier performances if I remember correctly. I came out to see it. I was dating what's his name – Joe – who played Brick. That doesn't make any sense, I'm a lesbian. Maybe I was dating the lighting designer.

ALISON. Kay Fein.

JAYNE. I was dating Kay Fein. No, that's no good, she was probably an archeologist at the time. I was there in Phoenix – doing something else. Or I was playing Mae. That's perfect. Simon and I were working together. And I was dating Kay. She *was* a lighting designer then. Or are Kay and I ever in the same city together?

SIMON. It doesn't matter.

JAYNE. I'm sorry. I interrupted. But she *can* be over the top sometimes. Alex. So cartoony. And talk about chewing the scenery. I've seen her use a curtain rod for a toothpick. I love her give her my love.

SIMON. Anyway we have met, it's nice to meet you again.

ALISON. Likewise.

SIMON. Looking forward to working with you.

HAL. Simon's playing Touchstone.

SIMON. "And as cast." Whatever that means.

HAL. I'll tell you in a minute. *(introducing* SIMON *to* ALEX-ANDRA*)* And this is Harry Samson.

SIMON. *(offering his hand)* Simon Lanquish.

HAL. And everybody knows Eve.

SIMON. Eve.

EVE. Addaman.

ALEX, ALISON, JAYNE, & SIMON. Addaman?

EVE. Eve. Eve Addaman.

ALEX, ALISON, HAL, JAYNE, & SIMON. Eve Addaman.

ALEX. More of the cast is coming up later?

HAL. Oh, that's what I was going to tell you. I have this idea, I'm going to do – being doing the play – with only four actors.

JAYNE. What?

ALISON. Only four?

SIMON. Is that what you meant by "and as cast?"

HAL. I have this idea. I'm going to be doing some doubling. And then I'll fill in the rest of the cast with some local actors. Local people.

(*The actors stare blankly.*)

I think I can keep the cast down to ten. It'll be more than just the four of you. You'll all be playing most of the major roles – some of you will. And then we'll have some local folks playing roles – make it kind of a community event. And Eve's gonna play a role also.

(**EVE** *holds up her hand.*)

EVE. I'm playing Adam, the old man.

JAYNE. That's interesting.

HAL. Now you guys need to deal with your luggage and where you're staying, right?

JAYNE. (*as Celia*) I cannot go no further.

HAL. Wait, back up further.

JAYNE. I'm confused. Have we just arrived, or have we been here for a while?

HAL. (*after a brief hold*) What do you mean?

JAYNE. (*to* **ALISON**) Because you say, This…Well, this is the Forest of Arden.

SIMON. Where are we?

HAL. Right.

JAYNE. (*pointing in the script for* **SIMON**) Here, honey. Rosalind, Alison, disguised as Ganymede.

HAL. That's right.

SIMON. I see.

JAYNE. So we've just arrived.

HAL. That's right.

JAYNE. In Arden.

HAL. Yea, I think so.

(HAL *looks to* EVE, *who nods.*)

JAYNE. *(as Celia)* I pray you bear with me, I cannot go no further.

SIMON. *(as Touchstone.)* For my part, I had rather bear with you, than bear you.

HAL. Good, okay. Make sense.

JAYNE. Yea.??? But it's a double negative, isn't it – cannot go no further. Why don't I just say, I cannot go further, or I can go no further? Am I really saying, I can go further?

HAL. *(consulting the text.)* I pray you, bear with me, I cannot go no further – I don't think so. I think you're just saying you can – you can't go any further – but you say, I cannot go no further – I think that's just how she says it. I think that's the way you talk.

EVE. It's archaic.

HAL. Right. Just as the way we speak may seem – will seem archaic – confusing – you know in a hundred years – or three hundred years. Or even now. The way we talk.

JAYNE. That's what I love about Shakespeare. It's like a foreign language. Not like Chekhov, where everything is spelled out.

HAL. Un huh. *(after a brief pause)* Okay, great. Why don't we take a break.

EVE. Ten minutes.

JAYNE. *(to ALISON – with girlish excitement)* It's going so well. Don't you think?

HAL. *(to EVE)* This day's a disaster.

ALISON. *(to JAYNE)* I think so.

JAYNE. *(spotting SIMON exiting, lighting up a cigarette)* Simon, I'll go with you. *(as they exit)* Honey, you shouldn't be smoking.

(ALISON *sits near* ALEXANDRA. EVE *and* HAL *confer.*)

ALEX. Hi there.

ALISON. Hi.

ALEX. How's it going?

ALISON. Okay. I think. How does it look?

ALEX. Okay. It's very early. You're doing well though.

ALISON. You think?

ALEX. Oh, yea.

ALISON. Do I seem like a musical comedy actress up there?

ALEX. What's a musical comedy actress?

ALISON. I don't know, superficial, artificial.

ALEX. No.

ALISON. I'm trying not to act.

ALEX. What do you mean?

ALISON. Like a boy.

ALEX. Like a boy?

ALISON. I mean…I am.

ALEX. Right.

ALISON. Trying to pretend – I am this woman and how she would…

ALEX. Yes.

ALISON. Disguise herself.

ALEX. Un huh.

ALISON. I don't know what I'm saying. Not…act it, but… just…kind of…act. Pretend. Behave.

ALEX. That sounds good.

ALISON. All the musicals I've been in over the years I've watched others – they won't relax – it's not that they're – that the *material* is artificial – it is of course – but that *they* are. These performers. And I've worked so hard at it. And thought so what it's only in a musical – what does it mean what would it mean in a play – not that I'm ready for Ibsen – but this –

ALEX. A comedy.

ALISON. Yes. Light.

ALEX. But serious.

ALISON. Yes. There's more – he's a genius – to it. But the principle applies. And that's the thing. One of the things. About my relationship. With Alex.

ALEX. Your ex-lover.

ALISON. *(startled by the "ex")* What? *(recovering)* Oh right – ex-lover. That she would never appreciate, or understand – what I was trying to accomplish. In the form. I mean she would compliment me – try to be helpful. But she judged the form, not the content. Or at least not the content of me.

ALEX. I see.

ALISON. *(after a pause)* I'm gonna get my hair cut for this. A buzz cut.

ALEX. A buzz cut?

ALISON. Think I could look like a boy?

ALEX. I don't know, what does a boy look like?

ALISON. Not like a girl.

ALEX. Oh right. But you don't want to look too much like a boy.

ALISON. Why not?

ALEX. Well, half the fun is knowing, you know, you're a girl – a woman.

ALISON. Really? For who?

ALEX. That you're a woman? Unh, I don't know, the audience, I suppose. Orlando.

ALISON. You think Orlando knows Rosalind is really a woman?

ALEX. I don't know – yet. I'd like to think he doesn't, but I'm not sure. Or maybe he's not sure.

ALISON. That's one of the things I like about what you're doing.

ALEX. What's that?

ALISON. It was odd when Hal cast you. I thought…I mean I enjoyed your audition. It was fun.

ALEX. Un huh.

ALISON. I guess I thought though you weren't my vision of what an Orlando should be.

ALEX. What did you have in mind?

ALISON. I don't know. I guess someone a bit…straighter.

ALEX. You don't think I'm straight?

ALISON. *(laughing)* No, I mean…Well, you know Hubert – who was going to be playing the part…he's very… masculine – and –

ALEX. I'm not masculine.

ALISON. No, I mean – this is not coming out right – but – like – when you called the other day about having dinner after rehearsal.

ALEX. Un huh.

ALISON. Which I really enjoyed by the way. I mean for a minute I thought – when I picked up the phone – and this is not a criticism – I thought it was a woman on the other end.

ALEX. Huh.

ALISON. I mean, has anyone ever –

ALEX. Because I have a high voice?

ALISON. Yea, I mean, you know, I think you're – I could see like…I'm losing language. I once saw a production of this play?

ALEX. *This* play.

ALISON. The one we're doing, right. And there were two guys – one was playing Rosalind – but he didn't do it in drag – just a suggestion of something. It was wonderful – a wonderful production. Most of the audience walked out. And both the guys were good-looking guys, but the Orlando was particularly…he wasn't beefy, but he seemed like a straight guy who maybe wasn't or maybe he was. With you…it's like – like when they did it, I knew who the man was and who the man wasn't, who the woman was – even though they were both men.

ALEX. Right.

ALISON. With you...I just don't think of you as...that kind of man.

ALEX. Sure.

ALISON. So it's different. I like it.

ALEX. Do you?

ALISON. Yea. It's not what I imagined. *(pause)* Can I ask you a personal question?

EVE. We're back.

ALEX. *(still looking at* **ALISON***)* Okay.

HAL. I want to try this idea I talked to you about the other day, Harry.

ALEX. *(to* **HAL***)* Un huh.

HAL. In the wrestling scene. And Simon.

SIMON. Right.

HAL. I'd like you to just throw the lines for Charles the wrestler to Harry. I know you're Touchstone. But just say the lines for Charles. And Harry. I want to see what it's like if you're kind of wrestling with yourself. You know what I mean? Grappling with yourself. So in other words there would be – there wouldn't be another actor you'd be struggling with – it would be yourself.

ALEX. Okay.

HAL. Can we try that?

ALEX. Sure.

HAL. Are you cool about doing this without your shirt?

ALEX. Oh sure. You want me to do that now?

HAL. If you don't mind. I want to see what it's like seeing you taking off your shirt.

ALEX. Okay.

HAL. You ready Simon?

SIMON. Yep.

HAL. Here we go. Down and dirty.

(**ALEXANDRA** *unbuttons her shirt, takes it off, begins wrestling, grappling, struggling with self.* **SIMON** *knocks on door.*)

ALEX. *(facing upstage, as if having released her breasts)* Who is it? *(That was a little high in the voice. Lower.)* Who is it?

SIMON. It's me, Simon.

HAL. You can even try bending over.

ALEX. *(to* **SIMON***)* Okay.

(**ALEXANDRA** *bends over, grabs shirt from floor, holds it up as if covering breasts.*)

HAL. *(to* **ALEXANDRA***)* Or get on your knees.

SIMON. Am I coming too early?

HAL. Do you want to use knee pads?

ALEX. *(to* **SIMON***)* No, it's fine.

(**ALEXANDRA** *feels under the pillow of bed, searching for Ace bandage.*)

HAL & SIMON. *(to* **ALEXANDRA***)* Are you sure?

ALEX. *(to* **SIMON***)* Yea.

HAL. *(to* **EVE***)* Why don't you get the knee pads for Harry. Look in the closet.

ALEX. *(momentarily abandoning search under pillow)* The closet.

EVE. *(to* **HAL***)* Where's the key?

ALEX. *(to* **SIMON***)* The what?

HAL. *(to* **EVE***)* Is it in your pants?

ALEX. *(to* **SIMON** *– feeling crotch)* What?

SIMON. *(to* **ALEXANDRA***)* I didn't say anything.

(**EVE** *finds key in pants.*)

EVE. *(holding up key)* Here it is, be right with you.

SIMON. *(to* **ALEXANDRA***)* Take your time.

HAL. *(to* **ALEXANDRA***)* Just take your time.

(EVE *exits.* ALEXANDRA *finds Ace bandage under other pillow.*)

ALEX. *(to* SIMON*)* Be right with you.

HAL. *(to* EVE*)* Eve, do you need some help with the door? *(to* ALEXANDRA*)* Hold on one sec.

(HAL *exits to* EVE, ALEXANDRA *exits to offstage bathroom with shirt and Ace bandage.*)

SIMON. Do you need some help with the door?

ALEX. *(from off)* Hold on one sec.

(ALEXANDRA *returns tucking shirt into pants. She adjusts her polyester penis.*)

(adjusting polyester penis) Come on, get over there, would ya. *(zipping pants, buckling belt)* Stupid thing, it's been in my way since the beginning.

(*As if before a mirror,* ALEXANDRA *touches chest, making sure bandage is secure. Flexes muscles. Final pouf of hair.* ALEXANDRA *opens door to* SIMON.*)*

Hey, buddy, come on in. Sorry.

SIMON. No problem. *(scanning* ALEXANDRA*)* What's up? Alex takes a furtive glance at groin. Checking to see theatrical member not rigidly misplaced into unwanted boner. This then macho slash gay-farcical opening of scene. Re-enter for different tack.

(SIMON *retreats, knocks.* ALEXANDRA *opens door to* SIMON.*)*

ALEX. Hi.

SIMON. Hi. Here then both characters evince shyness, Simon for reasons of attraction to Harry, Alex for fear of intimate discovery. This pseudo-ambiguous gay date-like opening of scene gives preferred flavor of possible male interaction.

ALEX. Sorry, just getting myself together.

SIMON. No problem. Here might say "adjusting your make-up, checking your eye-liner?" Or he perhaps, "just putting on my girdle," or better I to initiate effeminized remarks, "putting on your girdle, rip in your pantyhose?" He then to respond in kind, suggesting either conduct straight men might engage in with each other or with gay men or with women – gay or straight for reasons various; *or* it might suggest two gay men long accustomed to the habit of mocking women, women viewed inevitably inferior; this behavior real or imagined on the part of women a means for gay men to negotiate feelings of inferiority and insecurity. This tactic taken though the scene proceeds in unwanted direction. Simon no queen. Not given to queer innuendo.

Little behind?

ALEX. *(with hand on bottom)* I beg your pardon?

SIMON. Unnecessary to shun all forms of ribaldry. Some jokes consistent with light-hearted nature of entertainment. The "beg your pardon" line a clear reference to Ludlam's *Irma Vep*, certain to be appreciated by all those familiar with the piece.

You did say 7:30?

ALEX. Oh yea, no, you're right on time.

SIMON. Advance the plot with a scene of unwanted advance.

ALEX. Is Jayne meeting us?

SIMON. No, she's getting together with Alison?

ALEX. Jayne and Alison? Getting together?

SIMON. They may meet us later.

ALEX. What about Hal and Eve?

SIMON. I'm not sure what they're up to tonight. Day off tomorrow.

ALEX. Boy, I could use it.

SIMON. So could I. How will it play out? Does this scene foreshadow any unanticipated coupling? Couplings?

ALEX. Just us two then.

SIMON. Yea. Maybe.

ALEX. Let's go. Here we are. Little noisy – pooh, and smoky. Shall we get a booth? I'm starving. Yikes, that country music. I guess they don't have a no-smoking section. Oh, I forgot, you smoke. Anything without meat?

SIMON. If it bothers you I'll…

ALEX. Oh, don't worry about it.

SIMON. I should stop. You're a vegetarian?

ALEX. I try to be.

SIMON. I should have thought of another place, I'm sorry.

ALEX. It's all right, I'll find something, I didn't mention.

SIMON. They're sitting on the bed, as if at a table, holding empty glasses for props – or maybe just miming it. Local beer for Alex/Harry, gin and tonic for Simon.

ALEX. So Jayne and Alison went out together. That's interesting.

SIMON. What do you find interesting about that?

ALEX. About them going out together? Nothing. Nothing really. *(pause)* Where did they go?

SIMON. Dinner, I think. They were gonna take a walk together around the pond.

ALEX. At night? Together? Alison and Jayne?

SIMON. You seem very interested in Alison.

ALEX. Who me? In Alison? Why do you say that?

SIMON. You just do. I know you've been spending a lot of time together out of rehearsal.

ALEX. Just getting to know each other. Running lines. Getting acquainted.

SIMON. You know she doesn't like men.

ALEX. I do know that, yes. Absolutely.

SIMON. She split up with her lover recently.

ALEX. She mentioned something about that.

SIMON. Alexandra Page. I've worked with her.

ALEX. Oh right. I've heard she's an interesting actress.

SIMON. In the right thing. She's limited.

ALEX. Un huh. Well, we're all limited, I think – in our own way. I think.

SIMON. I didn't know them well – as a couple – but from what I heard – from Jayne – what Jayne heard – from somebody – I think it's very good for Alison. To be on her own. I don't think she's really had the chance to explore herself with Alexandra around.

ALEX. Yes, Alison intimated that.

SIMON. What about you?

ALEX. Have I explored myself?

SIMON. Are you involved with anyone? I heard you split up with someone recently.

ALEX. Yes, that was rough. But I think perhaps it's for the best.

SIMON. They nurse their drinks. You've been involved with mostly women?

ALEX. Almost exclusively.

SIMON. But not exclusively.

ALEX. When I was young – younger – not too young, I got a late start – so to speak – I did have a couple of experiences with men.

SIMON. Mm mm.

ALEX. I was attracted to women, but still afraid to…

SIMON. Did you like it?

ALEX. With men? Not enough to continue. Why do you ask?

SIMON. I was just…curious. You seem like…maybe you never met the right man.

ALEX. I don't think there is the right man. For me. *(pause)* What about you, Simon? Have you met the right man?

SIMON. Simon stares blankly.

ALEX. Are you okay? You've hardly touched your hamburger.

SIMON. I'm on a new medication. It's upsetting my stomach.

I broke up with the man I was seeing, I met him on Fire Island, we were together for nine months, it was a nightmare.

I met him at Splash, I met him at the Monster, he lives in my building, he goes to my gym. I met him online, I met him at church, we met at a party, he temps for my agent, we use the same laundry, I know him from group therapy, we're in the same running group, we met on the street. We get together we can't stop fighting, he says something I react, I think he's attacking me which he is in a way he thinks I'm being too judgmental or controlling, I get insulted, I get paranoid, we end up fighting, he went on tour so I proposed we stop seeing each other. What could he do but accept my proposal?

Plus I have AIDS. Which doesn't mean anything. It means something – which is why I shouldn't be smoking. My T-cells are good, my viral load is stable – for the most part. I also get testosterone injections to boost my immune system.

That's one way it could go. Or just oblique flirtation, confusion of sexes – given Alex's disguise. Nothing boiling over – like Jayne's always saying – mostly to myself. Let's forget this entire scene, shall we. I met Harry at his hotel room, we've had dinner, I'm drinking a little too much, I'm attracted to him, I'm a little desperate, I'm feeling that way, I'm out of town – it's easy to have a crush on another actor in that circumstance. Or at least it is for me.

Then Alison enters.

ALISON. Hi.

ALEX. Hi. Where's Jayne?

ALISON. I'm sorry?

ALEX. About what? I mean Jayne, Simon says –

SIMON. Simon says Jayne and Alison were having dinner.

ALISON. Oh right, and then we took a walk over to the lake.

ALEX. You mean the pond?

ALISON. The pond, yes.

SIMON. How was it?

ALEX. Where's Jayne?

ALISON. She got muddy.

ALEX. Jayne did?

ALISON. She was on the ground for a while. At the lake.

ALEX. You mean the pond.

(**ALISON** *pulls out a cell phone.*)

ALISON. *(pulling out her cell phone)* Do you mind if I call Alex? We haven't spoken today. I want to catch her in case she goes to bed early.

ALEX. You think she's home?

ALISON. Why wouldn't she be?

SIMON. I thought you and Alex split up.

ALISON. We still talk.

SIMON. Alex's cell phone rings.

ALEX. Oh, that's me. How funny.

ALISON. I'm trying her cell phone.

ALEX. Excuse me one second.

ALISON. You can stay here.

ALEX. It's all right. It might be my girlfriend.

SIMON. Your ex-girlfriend?

ALEX. We might need to talk about something.

ALISON. I wonder why she's not picking up?

SIMON. Alex crosses stage, goes into the men's room.

ALEX. Hello. *(That was a little low in the voice. Higher.)* Hello.

ALISON. Hi honey, it's me.

ALEX. Hi honey.

ALISON. Is this a good time?

ALEX. Oh sure.

ALISON. I thought I'd try you on your cell in case you were out.

ALEX. Oh no, I'm here.

ALISON. At home?

SIMON. Alex signals a guy he's not using the urinal.

ALEX. *(to guy)* Go 'head, no, I'm fine.

ALISON. What was that?

ALEX. Nothing, go ahead. How's it going up there?

SIMON. And then some stupid, comic, farcical dialogue.

ALISON. I've been spending a lot of time with him, he's a really nice guy.

ALEX. That's nice. Is he a good actor?

SIMON. Will she ever stop fishing? Let's fast forward.

ALISON. He's very attractive. I find myself strangely attracted to him.

ALEX. You mean like sexually?

ALISON. Well, I don't know, not really, kind of.

ALEX. Kind of? Sounds like you have a crush on him.

ALISON. Oh Alex, for goodness sake. I can understand you being jealous if I was spending time with another woman, but this guy is a guy.

SIMON. Toilet flushes.

ALISON. What was that?

ALEX. I'm in the subway.

ALISON. I thought you were at home.

ALEX. I'm coming home, going home, I'm on my way.

SIMON. Oh where were you? Seeing a show, a film, a movie, blah blah blah. Alex steps out of men's room, remains out of sight. Alison hears same country western song through phone she hears in restaurant.

ALEX. What a coincidence. I just walked past a bar, they must have the same station on.

SIMON. In New York, that they have in Maine?

ALEX. I'm so glad to know it's going well.

ALISON. It is, I'm feeling very good. I can't wait for you to see it.

ALEX. Oh, right. I have to make plans how to get up there.

SIMON. You'll hear about that in the final scene. Alex is slowly making her way back to the booth.

ALEX. Love you.

ALISON. Love you too.

SIMON. "Love you?" I'd never know the two of you split up.

ALISON. Yea, well we're – *(to ALEXANDRA)* Finish your phone call?

ALEX. Yea, my girlfriend.

SIMON. Alex sees somebody enter the restaurant.

ALEX. *(pointing)* Oh look.

SIMON. Alison's cell phone rings.

ALISON. *(into phone)* Hello.

ALEX. It's Jayne.

ALISON. *(into phone)* Hi Jayne.

SIMON. *(referring to the character that enters)* That's not Jayne.

ALEX. Who else could it be?

ALISON. *(into phone)* Oh Jayne, you won't believe it. Guess who just walked into the restaurant?

KAY. Hi troops.

ALISON. *(into phone)* Kay Fein.

ALEX. Oh. Kay. What are you doing here?

KAY. *(with meaning)* Do I know you?

ALISON. *(into phone)* I will. Did you get cleaned up?

ALEX. *(secretly to KAY)* I thought you were in Egypt, your hands filthy with the past.

ALISON. *(into phone)* You tripped, I know, I felt so bad. Well as long as you're okay.

KAY. *(with meaning)* Egypt?

ALEX. *(secretly to KAY)* Aren't you an archeologist?

KAY. *(to SIMON)* I think I'm a lighting designer.

SIMON. I think so too.

ALEX. Oh, right. I'm thinking of a different Kay. I must be thinking of a different Kay.

ALISON. Hi Kay.

KAY. Hi doll. *(kissing)*

ALISON. Great to see you.

KAY. *(to ALEX)* And you're…

ALEX. Harry.

KAY. *(seeing ALEXANDRA's hairy arms)* I know.

ALEX. Samson.

KAY. *(wryly)* Harry Samson?

ALISON. *(into phone, but with glance toward KAY and ALEXANDRA)* Uh huh.

KAY. *(secretly to ALEXANDRA)* How's it going?

ALISON. *(into phone, but with glance toward KAY and ALEXANDRA)* Okay.

ALEX. *(secretly to KAY)* Fine.

SIMON. Harry's playing Orlando. He replaced Humé Hubert.

ALISON. *(handing phone to KAY)* Here. Say hello.

KAY. *(into phone)* Hello? Hi Jayne. Long time no see. I just got here.

ALISON. *(to ALEXANDRA)* They used to see each other.

ALEX. I see.

KAY. *(into phone)* Oh, I'd love to see you. Would that be possible? Why not?

SIMON. Tell her to come over.

KAY. *(to SIMON)* She says she can't. *(into phone)* I see. Right now? Well where are you? Off stage?

ALEX. *(to KAY)* That's the name of the hotel.

KAY. *(to ALEXANDRA)* Oh how clever. *(into phone)* The Off Stage Hotel, I think I can find it. Do you want to talk to Alison again? See you soon. *(closing phone, to group)* She's lonely, she wants some company. I just hope we don't have a scene. That would be impossible. I'll take my chances. I'll pick up some pizza. I'll see you guys later.

(KAY exits.)

SIMON. A few more drinks – for Simon. His sad life. The girls listen. Alison and Alexandra.

ALEX & ALISON. We're women, not girls.

SIMON. He starts lines from the play. Lines of Touchstone.

ALEX. We gotta get him back to his room.

ALISON. Here, give me the check, can you get him outside?

ALEX. I think so. Do you need any money?

ALISON. Oh no, it's all right. Alex never has any money. I'm used to paying the check.

(**ALISON** exits.)

SIMON. Alexandra shoulders Simon to the exit. That cool night air in Maine.

ALEX. Slowly, Simon, one step at a time.

SIMON. A full sky of stars, not like what you see in the city. They'll make their way beneath this heavenly blanket.

ALEX. We gotta wait one second for Alison.

SIMON. I want to sleep with you Harry. I want to have sex with you.

ALEX. You may think you do sweetheart, but believe me, it's not gonna be worth your while.

SIMON. I find it sexy when a straight guy calls me sweetheart.

ALEX. Why the hell would you wanna have sex with a straight guy, Simon?

SIMON. I know. I don't know. I just do. I always have. You wanna sleep with Alison, don't you, and she's not straight.

ALEX. I find Alison attractive, but I'm not making any moves on her. Do you need to take any more medications tonight, Simon?

SIMON. Don't remind me. Shit. No, I'm done for the night. Only with meals.

(**ALISON** enters. Her hair is short. A boyish cut.)

ALISON. Hi, sorry. They were running my card.

ALEX. What happened to your hair?

ALISON. It's cut for the show. You think it's too short?

ALEX. No, it looks good. Let's go.

SIMON. If I was laying on the couch in my sparsely furnished hotel room – as I will be tomorrow on my day off – staring out at a small patch of sky and a jutting of trees, morosely going mad in the middle of the afternoon, lonely out of town, refusing to call my therapist, this is what I would be thinking.

Who needs a play about a gay man who occasionally drinks too much – with AIDS no less? Who needs another play about him?

ALISON. Are you sure this is the way, Harry?

ALEX. Positive. Pretty sure.

SIMON. Who needs a play about a gay man who's entered into a series of failed relationships and finds as he grows older he's drawn into relationships with younger and younger men? Who needs another play about him?

ALISON. I think we've covered this ground already, Harry.

ALEX. Trust me.

SIMON. Who needs a play about a gay man who gets turned on by straight men and can't even go to a gym because he might try to pick somebody up and once got punched in the face for trying and could never go back to that gym again? Who needs another play about him?

ALISON. This is getting scary, Harry. I think we're going into the woods.

ALEX. Believe me, I've been here.

SIMON. Who needs a play about a gay man who attends meetings for sexually compulsive behavior and goes right from those meetings to a bar or a bookstore or the pier or a men's room in the subway? Who needs another play about him?

ALEX. Keep going.

SIMON. Who needs a play about a gay man who dreamed of being a fine actor and of one day leading a troupe that would bring Shakespeare to minority children finding himself on his forty-sixth birthday trying to seduce a fifteen year old hispanic kid outside of Splash, pleading with the kid to come home and have sex with him and even though he himself has had twenty years of therapy is shocked when the kid says, go home with you alone to your apartment you might try to kill me, what do you think, I'm crazy, man? Who needs a play about him?

ALISON. Oh, I think I know where we are.

SIMON. Who needs a play about a gay man so fearful of what life holds he can't get out of bed in the morning, the recess under his quilt the closest he can get to either the womb or the grave? Who needs a play about him?

Who needs a play about an aging homosexual who's had and has – thank you very much – issues with his mother and I'm sorry we've gone over the terrain before but let's face it when you grow up in the home of the oppressor in this society who the hell do you think you're going to identify with more, a man or a woman! and Jesus Christ, who doesn't have issues with their mother? Who needs another play about him?

Who needs a play about a gay man who fucked up as he is goes to the theatre and sees one quote end quote positive image of gay people after the other acting like the biggest fucking queers in the world – or worse a singing transvestite in a supposedly serious musical who dies from AIDS and comes back from the dead – and funny that never happened to any of my friends! – making the same damn hair dresser jokes they've been making since the day one – "those brave and idiosyncratic characters who were here before AIDS and will be here when it's over-" and women from Westchester with too much make-up who look like drag queens themselves laughing their asses off or crying at this shit beside men in Levis and pink and powder blue sweatshirts with one ear ring laughing and crying just the same, but that's what masochism is I suppose, victory in defeat, and one of the reasons this fucked up man is in the audience is because he has an audition for this stupid play on Monday – and wants the goddamn fucking job – and who imagining the accolades he'll receive for his performance fucks up his audition so badly he doesn't even get a call back? Who needs another play about him?

ALEX. Come on Simon, we're almost there.

SIMON. Who needs a play about a man who's thrown seventy-five percent of his life away, squandered opportunity after opportunity and finds himself in middle-age the stereotype of a self-loathing homosexual, the only difference being that he doesn't camp it up? Who needs a play about him?

ALEX. Simon, we're in the hotel. But where is your key? I can't find your –

SIMON. God have mercy, god have light,
Get me through this goddamn night.
Night follows night follows every tomorrow,
What man doesn't deal with, man has to swallow.
Who needs another play about him?
Who needs another play about him?
Who needs another play about him?
Who needs another play about him?
Who needs another play –

ALEX. What did you say, Simon? Did you say something?

SIMON. What? Nothing, oh sorry, I was thinking to myself. I don't know where it is – the key.

ALEX. *(to ALISON)* Let's bring him to my room. *(to SIMON)* Simon, you're going have to sleep on my couch.

ALISON. Why don't we just get the manager to open his room?

ALEX. Well for one thing it's a plot device to get you and Simon into my room. But if you want to be a stickler about it, there's nobody at the desk after eleven.

ALISON. Right, we'd have to wake somebody up. And they're so grumpy here.

SIMON. I'll be fine on the couch. I hate to put you out, Harry. And I apologize for what I said before. And about you and… *(with a glance at* ALISON*)*

ALEX. It's all right.

ALISON. What's that mean?

ALEX. Nothing, come on. I'm just down the hall.

(Enter HAL *and* EVE.*)*

HAL. It's a little rough –

EVE. Us being lovers –

HAL. Her working as my assistant.

EVE. They've returned to the hotel after dinner, entered their room. Tomorrow they plan to take a drive, have a picnic near a lake. Some time alone together.

HAL. She's worked – been working as my assistant –

EVE. One of his assistants on a number –

HAL. On a few of my films – as one of my assistants – which is kind of rough, you know, kind of male-female power thing in a way – according to her – which I can understand.

EVE. They've taken off their coats – it grew chilly on the walk home, he's gone into the bathroom to pee, the sound of his urine hitting the porcelain, she's taken from her coat pocket several stones and a pine cone she collected on the walk home, places them on the wood floor, examines them, arranges them. When he returns he'll ask her are those the rocks you got on the way home. Yes and the pine cone.

HAL. And – you know, that was one thing – and then I got this call from a friend of mine –

EVE. This friend of his – Charlotte – she'd taken over this theatre space and she asked him –

HAL. She asked me about coming up directing a play –

EVE. Which he'd never done before.

HAL. And I'm working on the financing for a new film I want to do –

EVE. A play – funny, I've had more experience in the theatre than he has –

HAL. She comes from a dance-choreography background –

EVE. And as an actress –

HAL. She goes into the bathroom. He never hears or rather rarely hears her on the toilet. For one thing she closes the door, which he rarely does. Never does. And besides, he's picked up his cell phone checking his messages. His DP – he thinks of him as his DP, Alan, has called, left a message he wants to talk. He calls him, leaves a message to call him tomorrow anytime, forgets they have plans to have a picnic. Toilet flushes, well at least he knows when she's through. He sometimes forgets to flush the toilet, never mind putting the seat down. She returns hears him on the phone.

EVE. Cell phone. Pine cone.

HAL. She says to herself.

EVE. And I needed the money –

HAL. Well she didn't really need the money – but we thought –

EVE. We thought about traveling in the southwest, this summer – planned, actually, to go before Charlotte called and asked him to come up –

HAL. Asked me if I was interested in coming up, directing *As You Like It.*

EVE. He wanted to do it – he didn't really want to go to the southwest, that would have been more for me.

HAL. Both of them are in the bathroom now, brushing their teeth, playfully – but what is playfully? – pushing each other away from the mirror.

EVE. And they're talking about nothing much by now, regressing as they often do before bed, taunting each other in childish ways, teasing one another, venting their hostilities obliquely, she laughing more than he, he having a talent to amuse, both of them hurt by the other's remarks, it all a game, empty.

HAL. So she figured –

EVE. I figured I didn't want to go to the southwest alone –

HAL. Which I proposed –

EVE. And I could – I suppose – use the money, so he –

HAL. I offered her like to work as my assistant, stage manager, prop mistress-kind-of-everything-person, you know, so she wouldn't – we wouldn't be separated all summer – or for most of the summer.

EVE. They're undressed by now. I'm in my late twenties, she's thinking, he's in his early thirties. Pine cone, cell phone.

HAL. What'd you say?

EVE. Pine cone, cell phone.

HAL. What's that about?

EVE. Nothing.

HAL. And when the show goes up, I'll go back to New York, see if I can close up some of the financing for the new film – and she'll –

EVE. I'll stay here, run the performances.

HAL. So I think she's a little frustrated – because she'd like – what she'd like to be doing –

EVE. Is making films of my own.

HAL. She's not really interested in the theatre.

EVE. Though I come from this dance-choreography background. My mother was a choreographer.

HAL. She's got a lot of issues with her mother.

EVE. I've made two films.

HAL. Interesting experimental short kind of films about light, very different…difficult…different from mine.

EVE. Very different from Hal's.

HAL. They've made love. Now they're cuddled up together in spoons. The stars outside the window.

EVE. So you see how it all –

HAL. It's kind –

EVE. It's been difficult. And I haven't said much – to anyone, about it. But. Well.

HAL. They have a fight the next morning.

EVE. It's very complicated.

HAL. Women and men and women.

EVE. Very complicated

HAL. Very complicated.

EVE. Good night, sweetheart.

HAL. Good night, sweetheart.

(They're in bed by now.)

ALEX. Okay, here we are. Moving on. Easy Simon.

SIMON. I'm okay.

ALISON. Harry, there's no couch.

ALEX. What?

ALISON. There's no couch. Where is Simon going to sleep?

SIMON. Yea, where am I going to sleep?

ALEX. Oh right, there's no couch. I forgot.

ALISON. He can sleep in the bed with you.

ALEX. *(indicating* HAL *and* EVE *in bed)* There won't be room.

ALISON. Oh right.

ALEX. *(to* SIMON*)* I guess you'll have to sleep on the floor.

SIMON. Well, how about if I sit in a chair and pretend I'm sleeping on the floor?

ALEX. *(after thinking about it)* That's fine.

(He does so – sits off to the side.)

ALISON. You have a nice room, Harry. My god, you have a kitchenette.

ALEX. It's an efficiency.

ALISON. None of the other rooms in the hotel have one.

ALEX. I know – there's a big joke near the end of the scene – I needed a garbage disposal.

ALISON. That's so nice. *(She's close to him.)* Harry. Your arms are so hairy.

ALEX. I know.

ALISON. I'm attracted to you, Harry. Did you know that?

ALEX. Uh huh.

ALISON. Are you attracted to me? I think you are.

ALEX. Of course, I am. You're a beautiful woman. And I'm a man. I've dreamt of having you in my arms.

ALISON. Oh.

ALEX. But Alison. You're on the rebound. I don't want you using me like some kind of sex toy.

ALISON. It's funny. I'm not usually attracted to men.

ALEX. Usually? What does that mean?

ALISON. It's funny. I've never been attracted to a man before.

ALEX. And my girlfriend and I, we're…kind of in a strange place with each other…right now. I've got to be careful.

ALISON. There's something soft and gentle about you Harry. You're not just some stupid stud.

ALEX. Well, I hope not.

(They kiss.)

Oh, Alison.

(They kiss again.)

I'm in love with you. I've been in love with you since we first met.

ALISON. Then why don't you ever show it?

ALEX. I have difficulty with my feelings.

*(**ALISON** touches **ALEXANDRA**'s chest.)*

Oh, don't touch me there. I'm very sensitive there. Are you wearing a bandage? I had a slight injury. Your arms are a little sticky. I don't know how to explain that. The fact of the matter – and then of course there's Simon laying on the floor here.

*(Indicating where **SIMON** is not, **SIMON** waves a hand from his seat.)*

ALEX. What if he should wake up? With all that's going on, I'm concerned I might not be able to perform properly. I mean I'm sure I would. I'm an attractive man.

ALISON. You are. You're cute. You're sweet. I bet women go crazy over you.

ALEX. Some do.

ALISON. Let's turn off the lights.

(The lights dim.)

(as if to the lighting booth) Thank you.

(You know who enters in pajamas. **HAL** *and* **EVE** *sit up in bed to watch.* **ALEXANDRA** *and* **ALISON** *stand to the side.)*

JAYNE. Oh Kay, that was wonderful.

ALEX. A scene, of course, between Kay Fein and Jayne Summerhouse.

KAY. Jayne, I can't believe I let you talk me into that.

JAYNE. Kay, I didn't talk you into anything? Did you or did you not tell Charlotte you were hoping we'd have some kind of reunion when you got up here?

KAY. And she told you?

JAYNE. Since when has Charlotte ever kept a confidence? You knew the minute you told her the first thing she was going to do was tell me. That's probably why you told her in the first place.

KAY. Well I'll say one thing about you Jayne…You know, I think we should start the scene over. It means a whole different thing if we've had sex.

JAYNE. *(disappointed)* All right, fine.

KAY. And another thing completely if we haven't. Sex is so easy.

JAYNE. Speak for yourself. That was good pizza. Thank you for bringing that over, Kay.

KAY. My pleasure.

JAYNE. I can't believe I let you talk me into it, though You know I have to watch my weight.

KAY. Jayne, you're always talking about your weight. You look fine. You look terrific. Stop fishing for compliments.

JAYNE. It's so good to see you Kay. I've missed you. When Charlotte told me you were coming up I was so excited.

KAY. You're studying film.

JAYNE. Yea. And.

KAY. Well, isn't that something.

JAYNE. Do you want to have a conversation about it?

KAY. Well, wouldn't it be a good way to get reacquainted, talk about our lives?

JAYNE. And you'll talk to me about your work as an archeologist or a lighting designer?

KAY. Something like that.

JAYNE. We'll review the specifics of our history together or not together. Reminisce how we met, where we met. Spend these precious moments we have together in idle chit chat.

KAY. I don't consider these things necessarily idle.

JAYNE. Let's cut to the chase, Kay. If this were a play, do you think an audience would want to sit through the back story, the exposition.

KAY. Fine.

JAYNE. Why didn't things work out between us, Kay?

KAY. Damn it. I knew the minute I walked in here we'd have a scene.

JAYNE. Well that's what life is, Kay. Scenes. One after the other. Episodes, chapters, events. You never know how it's going to play out. Two women who haven't seen each other for years, both single – still – approaching middle age – fine, arrived at.

KAY. One of them, or so I heard from Charlotte – who's taken steps to change her life, going back to school –

JAYNE. Yes, the money I stowed away from the soap to study film. And dumped that god awful therapist –

KAY. The one that kept telling you to seek your goodness, discover your flower, open yourself to munificence? That was money well spent.

JAYNE. Now I'm seeing Simon's therapist – he tells me how narcissistic I am, how self-involved – what about discovering my flower, opening myself to goodness – he practically guffaws in my face.

KAY. Uh huh.

JAYNE. Uh huh? What about you Kay, are you a cipher? Say something about yourself.

KAY. Cipher? You know next to Alexandra Page you are the most abrasive woman I have ever known.

JAYNE. Known? You mean like in the biblical sense? I always knew there was something between you and Alexandra.

KAY. And here we have a demonstration of your paranoia – if you're even being serious – or of your inclination to melodrama. That's a trait you and Alex have in common. I never slept with Alex – I never had any interest in sleeping with Alex – nor to the best of my knowledge has she did she ever have any interest in me – in that way –

JAYNE. Yea – well –

KAY. You've always had this some kind of odd rivalry with Alex – this competition. Which was ridiculous. For all your shenanigans, Alex was never half the actress you are – you know it and she knows it. You've worked much more than she has – and got paid for it more than she has.

JAYNE. Not that that necessarily means –

KAY. It doesn't mean everything, it sometimes doesn't mean anything, but in this case at least it means something. And how dare you – dare you even Jayne –

JAYNE. Little more pizza?

KAY. Shut up for a minute and don't change the subject.

JAYNE. *(in coloratura)* Wha–?

KAY. You have an awful habit of doing that, Jayne. Besides, you don't need any more pizza. You can ill afford the calories.

JAYNE. *(as an intake of breath)* Ahh!

KAY. For you to accuse me of infidelity. You – and talk about your – there's another example of your rivalry with Alexandra – flirting with Alison –

JAYNE. I haven't seen Alison for years until –

KAY. You know what I mean. And the promiscuity – or the attempt at it – before I met you and after we split.

JAYNE. Well, I'm sorry Kay. Unlike you I don't live in the past. I did feel – I still feel – shit – that women – I'm a woman – and we should have the right to explore ourselves sexually just as much as any man. I want – I wanted – I'm older now – I wanted – I still want – the prerogative ascribed to men, not to be tied down exclusively to one person for my entire life. People have affairs. You know it as well as I do. The heterosexual construct of marriage is a no win situation.

KAY. What do you mean by marriage? Monogamy?

JAYNE. Of course.

KAY. Well when it comes to heterosexuals, monogamy is a relatively recent innovation.

JAYNE. Isn't that just like you, Kay, to throw around your weight as an archeologist.

KAY. *(devilishly)* Let's not start talking about weight.

JAYNE. *(fuming)* You can't live up to it and nobody or at least nobody I know – that we know – does – ever does.

KAY. Alex and Alison do.

JAYNE. Yes! and they split up.

KAY. I don't know anything about that. I've not been in any of those scenes. The point is – despite their problems – which are many – they have stayed together – now I realize that's complicated because the reasons some people do stay together – well, it's complicated.

JAYNE. Dependency. Alison is –

KAY. Granted, unhealthy forms of dependency – but it's not been all bad – and they do struggle – hell, they've stayed together longer than most of the straight couples we know.

JAYNE. What's your point, Jayne?

KAY. Kay. I'm Kay – you're Jayne.

JAYNE. What? Oh, shit. This is so confusing.

KAY. What *was* my point? This perpetual tangentia. Oh, yes – not living up to the heterosexual construct of marriage. See – you're laughing – the minute I repeat it you know how ridiculous that is. I mean the sight of you that evening, Jayne, with a cigarette in one hand and a light beer in the other standing in the crowd outside The Cubby Hole. If you knew how ludicrous –

JAYNE. They happen to have a very nice vegetarian menu.

KAY. You were eating a burger.

JAYNE. I needed the protein.

KAY. You sure as hell didn't need those french fries.

JAYNE. It came with the order.

KAY. Jayne, the only people who advocate fluid relationships are the ones that can't tolerate solid ones. Look at Charlotte – she spouts the same baloney. Well Charlotte hasn't had a long-term relationship since Winnie-the-Pooh. Now she's into "Asian" men – and excuses it with multiculturalism.

JAYNE. You moved away from me.

KAY. From you? How do you move away from somebody who's always on the prowl. "I want to be a wolf. I have desires-"

JAYNE. I said that when I was younger.

KAY. Why would any person in their right mind, Jayne – man or woman – want to claim the male prerogative? It's one of the most unfortunate developments since the stone age – or before – even if it did have its evolutionary moment or two. It makes you think that god really is a man. Who but a man would be stupid enough to create male behavior? And believe me, I have no investment in the matriarchy. That's as much of a dead end as the other. The priestess of the moon humping the phallus of the adolescent sacrifice.

JAYNE. *(on the verge of tears)* I was just having a beer.

KAY. Honey, it's as old as Abraham throwing Sarah to the pharaoh.

JAYNE. Now you stop right there, Kay. I may not be observant, but I am of the Jewish persuasion. Please do not besmirch the reputation of the patriarch.

KAY. Just because you initiate a religion doesn't mean you can't be a schmuck every once in a while.

JAYNE. Oh cut him some slack, Kay. He came from Sumeria. He never had the benefits of a religious education.

KAY. Well now we're just being silly.

JAYNE. Now? *(after a pause)* I've missed our fights, Kay. There's nothing like a good fight.

KAY. *(gently – but seriously)* Mrs. Molloy. *The Matchmaker.* You can't fool me, I lit you when you did it.

JAYNE. Oh right. I guess you did.

KAY. Come on, Jayne. Let's not get sentimental here.

JAYNE. *(after a pause)* Okay. Fine.

(EVE *and* ALISON *move from their respective positions, take stools, sit beside each other down right.)*

ALISON. What now ensues at this the peripeteic stage of the drama?

EVE. In answer: the requisite scene of sexual farce between Alexandra and Alison.

ALISON. What sight first greets the audience as this the penultimate scene unfolds?

EVE. Alison pulling Harry towards the bed.

ALISON. Describe the threat of intense physical compromise to which Alexandra now anticipates being made subject.

EVE. The descent of Alison's hand in the direction of the artificial groin.

ALISON. What tack does Alexandra employ to prevent contact with that aforementioned hand?

EVE. Interception. Meeting that hand with her own in the region of her navel, she deftly removes it to her lips.

ALISON. What tender words does she enunciate upon the kissing of that sweet hand?

EVE. Uh, Alison?

ALISON. And Alison's response?

EVE. Harry.

ALISON. What next occurs?

EVE. Placing her left hand on the back of Alison's head, bringing their mouths together, Alexandra engages Alison in a manner worthy of Belmondo.

ALISON. What phrase might best describe the purpose of Alexandra's maneuver?

EVE. An effort to buy some time.

ALISON. Given the moment of opportunity, what action does Alexandra perform?

EVE. Maintaining a steady and enjoyable swishing of tongues, holding still the back of Alison's head in her left hand, she dips her right hand into the cavity of her back pocket.

ALISON. What thought occurs to Alexandra as she proceeds in this fashion?

EVE. She wonders if Alison thinks he's taking out protection.

ALISON. And is she?

EVE. In a sense. Extracting her cell phone from the recess of her pocket, locating the appropriate button, she applies the appropriate pressure.

ALISON. And what happens?

EVE. Alison's cell phone rings.

ALISON. State concisely the successive events.

EVE. In brief: Alison detaches herself from Harry, removes her cell phone, flips it open, sees it is Alex who is calling and, with Harry's encouragement, repairs to the bathroom where she might converse with Alexandra in privacy.

ALISON. Given that this leads by means of shame and embarrassment to Alison's subsequent departure and jettison of the anticipated scene of sexual deception, outline the scene as initially imagined and reasons for its revision.

EVE. Again in brief: inspired by Singer's *Yentl,* the final subterfuge was to be accomplished by means of a candle, extinguished for maximum darkness, inserted in place of the prop penis, which given its flaccidity, was made pulver in the garbage disposal. Hence the need for the kitchenette. But this evoked an inevitable dilemma. It is one thing to deceive a woman with whom you desire no further contact, another a partner to whom you hope ultimately to return, and with whom you have enjoyed conjugal intimacy. Further, if the trickster evaporates at the end of the drama, good enough, but Alexandra is no disappearing act. She must live in the world, and as such must conduct herself accordingly. Thus Alison's removal became an absolute necessity, and is if I may say accomplished with commendable brevity.

SIMON. Staring at the door after Alison's departure, Alexandra hears the sigh of a recumbent Simon.

KAY. Grateful for four weeks out of town in which her off time was used at a local gymnasium, she lifts the sleeping figure from the floor and onto the bed.

ALEX. Turning back the sheets, she removes his shoes and socks, strips off his pants and shirt, folds them neatly, places them on a chair. She knows how horrible it is to wake in yesterday's clothes. His white briefs, the hair on his legs and back. So this is Simon. A real man.

EVE. What picture composes itself in Alexandra's mind – Simon's elevated rump before her?

ALEX. I like it when straight men call me sweetheart. His briefs pulled down, the candle in his ass.

SIMON. But what does Alexandra do?

ALEX. Pull up the sheet, brush the hair from his eyes, consider her own sins.

KAY. What sins are those?

ALEX. Too many to enumerate. It comes down, I suppose, to a lack of love.

HAL. What sight greets Alexandra as she moves from the bed to the window?

ALEX. The sky of stars. The peeping universe. At every moment we're watched. A million eyes. It sees what we do.

EVE. Does she sit now by the window?

ALEX. Yes and weeps. Her own life, the sleeping figure. Those of the comedy. And all the sleepers.

ALISON. Do some sleep in hunger?

ALEX. Yes.

ALISON. Do some sleep in fear?

ALEX. Yes.

ALISON. Do some sleep well?

ALEX. I suppose. A few.

ALISON. Do you? Do I? And how does the night proceed?

ALEX. Like an old woman in a dark dress, slowly trudging along. At first she was a young woman draped in indigo, now her steps falter as she approaches the dawn.

ALISON. Do you mean we're growing older?

ALEX. Oh, sweetheart.

KAY. Speak of the forms of comedy as you understand them.

ALEX. There is comedy, there is tragic comedy, comic farce and comic tragedy – and other permutations. Beckett I think was wrong, the master I think was wrong. His plays are comic tragedy not tragic comedy. For they end in despair.

SIMON. Do you propose the happy escape from misery?

ALEX. If only I could. Not how we behave but how we should behave.

HAL. What happens when the old woman stumbles?

ALEX. She falls into her grave. It's dawn.

KAY. And after that?

ALEX. Another day, another dollar. Another evening.

KAY. And how will that evening begin?

ALEX. With a new scene. You see, I'm always one step ahead of you.

ALISON. Alex, do you know what time it is? We're going to be late.

KAY. One question last?

ALEX. Yes.

KAY. Does Alison know of Alexandra's masquerade? Has she known from the very beginning?

ALEX. I can do no more than refer you to the reviews Lynn Fontaine received when she played Ilona in *The Guardsman*, the play on which this play is modeled. Ilona claims to have known all along it was her husband, Nandor, in disguise. There is this twinkle in her eye. But you're never quite sure what's behind that twinkle. *(to* ALISON*)* I'll be right out.

*(*ALEXANDRA *exits.)*

ALISON. You've been in that bathroom all night. What are you doing?

ALEX. Changing.

ALISON. Again?

ALEX. We've got plenty of time, keep your shirt on.

ALISON. It's so good to be home.

ALEX. I missed you this summer. It was hard your being away.

ALISON. I really appreciate your coming up to see the show.

ALEX. Oh, it was my pleasure. I wish I could have stayed longer – you know – more than one night. You were so good, I was so proud of you. I thought everybody was quite good. Jayne and Simon – and that young woman...

ALISON. Eve.

ALEX. Eve.

ALISON. Addaman.

ALEX. Addaman?

ALISON. Eve. Eve Addaman.

ALEX. Eve Addaman. She was very good.

ALISON. She ended up directing the play.

ALEX. You were telling me. Now tell the audience. But tell them as though you're telling me. That's how plays work every once in a while.

ALISON. Well, either Hal had to get back to New York all of a sudden because of financing for his film, or there was some big artistic emotional brouhaha and he left under less than agreeable circumstances.

ALEX. That's amazing.

ALISON. Or perhaps he left for a more plausible reason.

ALEX. Or maybe he didn't leave at all. Maybe it was amicable. Perhaps they ended up co-directing.

ALISON. She was amazing. I mean she stuck to Hal's original conception – basically – but she had – she just has a much better way with actors and she really understands the stage. And the changes she did make made everything make so much more sense. I guess the idea originally was Eve's anyway.

ALEX. Really? Well I thought it was terrific. And it was nice seeing Jayne. She was actually civil to me.

ALISON. I think Kay's being up there had a very nice influence on her.

ALEX. I'll say. It was great seeing them together. I never thought that would happen.

ALISON. Well, that's the magic of the theatre for you.

ALEX. And Simon. Poor Simon. I don't know what to say about him. *(pause)* Do we have any more exposition?

ALISON. That depends on how much longer you stay in the bathroom.

ALEX. Well, I want to look nice for Jayne's screening.

ALISON. It's just for her class up at Columbia.

ALEX. *A Pseudo-Documentary About Reality in the Theatre.* What an interesting title. I wonder what it's about? Ask me something about Kay.

ALISON. Will Kay be there this evening, or did she return to Egypt?

ALEX. I think from this point on, wherever you see Jayne you'll see Kay. She's finally decided that she is a lighting designer.

ALISON. Really?

ALEX. Yes. She says that archeology is a thing of the past.

ALISON. *(after a pause)* Uh huh. You know I wish you could have met Harry when you were up there.

ALEX. Oh yea, I would have loved to have met him. I really enjoyed his performance. Did you like working with him?

ALISON. He said he would meet us after the show. In fact, right after I left you at the box office, I went backstage to look for him. He was just getting to the theatre. I told him we'd all be getting together that evening and he said he'd join us. But then he never showed up at the restaurant. I guess his girlfriend – ex-girlfriend – girlfriend – came up that night. At least that's what he told me.

ALEX. Uh huh.

ALISON. I looked for you in the audience during the curtain call, I couldn't see you.

ALEX. Oh, I was there all right. And like I say, I really admired your work. You didn't push, acting like something that you weren't. It was clear and direct. I was inspired by what you did.

ALISON. Thank you, honey.

ALEX. And I liked what's his name too. The guy that played Orlando.

ALISON. Harry.

ALEX. Harry, right. I thought he was very good. *(pause)* What did you think of his performance?

ALISON. I thought he was all right.

ALEX. Um mm.

ALISON. But you know who I think would be really good in that role?

ALEX. Who?

ALISON. You.

ALEX. Me?

ALISON. Uh huh.

ALEX. Why do you say that?

ALISON. I don't know, I just have this feeling. And guess what?

ALEX. What?

ALISON. Hal has decided to revive the production this fall in New York.

ALEX. You're kidding.

ALISON. Eve is directing, Hal is producing. Jayne and Simon are doing it, they've asked me and I think they're going to ask…you.

ALEX. Me? I didn't think Hal liked my work as an actor.

ALISON. Oh, I think he sees things in you that perhaps he didn't see in the past.

ALEX. Uh huh. What about Eve? Does she – I don't even think she knows my work?

ALISON. I think she has some acquaintance with it.

ALEX. Uh huh.

ALISON. Simon and Jayne loved the idea.

ALEX. They did, huh?

ALISON. Kay had a few reservations initially, but I think –

ALEX. She now…too –

ALISON. Sees –

ALEX. Yes. Uh huh.

ALISON. Think about it honey. It would be a lot of fun to work on something together. Especially now that I'm more my own person. I think I could be helpful to you.

ALEX. I'll think about it.

ALISON. All right. But in the meantime stage time is very different from real time and we don't have any more time. It's either now or never. Enter in all your glory.

*(Enter **ALEXANDRA**. She is exactly as she was when we last saw her: i.e. the actor is* not *in drag.)*

ALEX. Here I am. How do I look?

ALISON. Just like yourself. Beautiful.

ALEX. Oh, please. *(giving **ALISON** her back)* Here, zip me up. *(Bending slightly and as though pulling her hair over her head to expose the zipper.)*

ALISON. You look good in this dress.

ALEX. I gotta lose some weight.

ALISON. I thought you said you cut your hair.

ALEX. Oh I did say that didn't I. *(turning to **ALISON**)* I look okay?

ALISON. Ravishing.

ALEX. Come on, you're the pretty one in this family.

ALISON. Your arms are so smooth. Did you get a waxing?

ALEX. Um hum.

ALISON. So smooth.

ALEX. *(quietly, directly)* I love you.

ALISON. *(quietly, directly)* I love you too. You will think about doing the play, won't you?

ALEX. Think about it? It's not like I have any other offer. And it would be nice to work together. Maybe we could help each other.

ALISON. Um hum.

ALEX. And a comedy. Life is so hard. It's so good to laugh. To make other people laugh.

(Pause. Then **ALISON** *exits.* **ALEXANDRA** *follows, stops, holds near the exit, speaks to the audience.)*

(to the audience) We're just pretending there's a door here. And I'm going to leave it open. I could close the door, but I think it's more interesting to leave it open. And besides, I trust you all completely.

*(***ALEXANDRA*** exits.)*

End of Play